Praise for Long

Dr. Gage and her son have written a book about a serious topic that affects so many lives, cancer. In so doing, they demonstrate not only the courage in confronting and dealing with difficult parts of our human journey, they have provided everyone a healing and positive path for coping with cancer. Perhaps, most poignant is the fact that the book is based on their personal story and how together they overcame the fear, anxiety, shame and other emotions so common to a cancer experience. Indeed, Dr. Gage and her son developed practical tools for communication, coping, and understanding when our loved one is diagnosed with cancer. Written from the perspective of a magical kingdom with a queen, king and others, this book engages the reader with excitement and interest while teaching children and professionals ways to confront, experience, embrace and ultimately overcome the negative emotions that cancer can bring. I am thrilled to recommend this needed read to children, counselors, teachers, and all adults, as our society continues to be so affected by this feared disease.

—Paul Nussbaum, Ph.D., ABPP,
President of the Brain Health Center, PA

Cancer. This word justifiably strikes fear, anxiety and uncertainty in adults. If such emotions plague adults, how is a child to deal with this scary diagnosis? *Long Live the Queen* is a book written by Dr. Gage and her son, who address these emotions head on and deliver invaluable guidance through clear, kindhearted storytelling. Read how the main character, Princess Isabella, handles her emotions surrounding her mother's cancer diagnosis and treatment with coping methods originating from invaluable professional experience and real-life studies. Dr. Gage delivers guidance to parents (and anyone who cares for children), advising how a child's development affects their understanding of cancer and how one should approach a child based upon their developmental stage. She shares her own struggles and triumphs during her tumultuous cancer scare. *Long Live the Queen* is essential for those recently diagnosed with cancer who need to share their story with a child. It is an indispensable book that dispels the confusion entailed with the diagnosis of cancer, giving knowledge, strength and confidence during an uncertain time.

—Dr. Gina Penaflor, M.D., FAAP, Pediatrician

I was very impressed with *Long Live the Queen* in that it helps children of all ages deal with their fears and worries about cancer treatment, as well as giving useful coping skills and tools for both children and parents to utilize during difficult times. We first meet a lovely royal family living in the imaginary kingdom of Groveth. When Queen Anna is diagnosed with cancer, her family and the entire kingdom are overwhelmed and fearful. As the story unfolds, we witness her children, Isabella and Philip, dealing with the physical and emotional deterioration of their mother from her illness and medical treatment. The journey ahead is a frightening one with an uncertain future. However, it serves as a useful vehicle to explore the need for honesty, communication, clarification, and trying to maintain some normalcy in an abnormal situation.

Children reading this story will have questions answered, fears allayed and most importantly they will be encouraged to discuss all of their concerns and worries. The fact that the outcome of the queen's treatment is somewhat uncertain paints a realistic picture, and while giving the reader hope it allows for more difficult scenarios. Following this engaging story are concise guides and strategies to help all members of the family deal with the challenges accompanying the diagnosis of cancer. It is truly a "family affair." Dr. Gage relates her own experience being diagnosed with cancer and the emotional impact it had on her spouse and sons. She has traveled this road herself and despite the trials and tribulations along the way, she and her son Christopher produced this book as a gift to all those who read it. Some of the questions addressed: What do I tell my kids? How should I tell them? What do I say to my children? Guidelines to answer these questions are broken down to a child's developmental age. A section on dealing with teenagers is also included. Keeping routines, when and how to tell others and what to tell them is clearly mapped out.

I highly recommend this book to anyone diagnosed with cancer in order to help them, their children and family members deal with such a stressful, lifetime event and challenge. Dr. Patricia Gage is a highly respected psychologist, community leader and most importantly a loving wife and mother who knows first hand how frightening a diagnosis of cancer can be. One of her concluding statements in the book is, "Yes, cancer may kill me, but I can also live." I hope this wonderful, well written and from the heart book will find a place in the homes, hospitals and institutions of all those who can use it and benefit from its wisdom.

—Richard E. LoSardo, M.D., Board Certified General Psychiatry,
Board Certified Child & Adolescent Psychiatry

An important contribution to the literature, written with sensitivity and wisdom. Dr. Gage speaks from the heart of a survivor and a professional.

Long Live the Queen is chock-full of advice, such as "You may want to check with your child's school to see if there is a guidance counselor or a school psychologist available for your child to talk to." I am so glad she states that by avoiding the word cancer, you are sending the wrong message. And I love the statement, "Yes, cancer may kill me, but I can also live." There are some real gems in here! The valuable, quick sources of information is a gift as well. *Long Live the Queen!* What a delightful way to help children.

—Judith L. Alpert, Professor of Applied Psychology, New York University, former President of Division of Trauma Psychology, American Psychological Association

Long Live the Queen

Help for Children Who Have a Loved One With Cancer

Patricia P. Gage, Ph.D. *and* Christopher J. Gage

Illustrations by Marlo Garnsworthy

Long Live the Queen: Help for Children Who Have a Loved One With Cancer
Copyright © 2020 by Patricia P. Gage, PhD, Christopher J. Gage,
and Marlo Garnsworthy

Paperback: ISBN: 978-1-7357393-0-4
eBook: ISBN 978-1-73557393-4-2

Library of Congress Control Number: 2020919270

Authors' Websites

Patricia P. Gage, Ph.D.: www.BrainSmartAcademics.com
Marlo Garnsworthy: www.IceBirdStudio.com

Published by

Brain Smart Academics, LLC
5 E. High Point Road
Stuart, Florida, 34996

Orders
Amazon.com

Original publication 2018 by Rainbow Books, Inc.
P.O. Box 430, Highland City, Florida 3346-0430
RainbowBooksInc.com

Photography Credits

Patricia Gage by Steven Martine Photography & Film
Christopher Gage by Patricia Gage
Marlo Garnsworthy by Carter Hasegawa/Long River Photography

All rights reserved. No part of this book may be reproduced or transmitted in any form or by any means, electronic or mechanical (except as follows for photocopying for review purposes). Permission for photocopying can be obtained for internal or personal use, the internal or personal use of specific clients, and for educational use, by contacting the publisher.

Disclaimer: *This book is for educational purposes only.* It is not meant to replace the expert care, advice and treatment of your health care provider. The information is designed to provide helpful information on the subjects discussed. It is not meant to be used to diagnose, or treat, any medical or psychological conditions. If you have any concerns, always seek professional medical advice from your doctor or mental health provider as soon as possible. The publisher and author are not responsible for any specific health needs that may require medical supervision and are not liable for any damages or negative consequences from any treatment, action, application or preparation, to any person reading or following the information in these guides. References are provided for informational purposes only and do not constitute endorsement of any websites or other sources.

Produced and Printed in the United States of America.

In grateful acknowledgment to

the extraordinary teams of medical professionals

in two medical centers for their endless compassion for their

patients,

unrelenting devotion and determination to the treatment of cancer:

Dr. Suzanne L. Wolden and Dr. David G. Pfister,

from Memorial Sloan Kettering Cancer Center,

and

Dr. Gary Griffis, Dr. José Suarez

and Dr. Nicholas O. Iannotti,

from the Cleveland Clinic Martin Health Robert and Carol

Weissman Cancer Center.

Contents

Acknowledgments . . . xi
Introduction . . . xiii

Long Live the Queen

    To the Young Reader . . . 21
    Chapter 1 . . . 25
    Chapter 2 . . . 29
    Chapter 3 . . . 23
    Chapter 4 . . . 37
    Chapter 5 . . . 43
    Chapter 6 . . . 47
    Chapter 7 . . . 51
    Chapter 8 . . . 57
    Chapter 9 . . . 61
    Chapter 10 . . . 65
    Chapter 11 . . . 71
    Chapter 12 . . . 77
    Chapter 13 . . . 81
    Chapter 14 . . . 87
    Chapter 15 . . . 91
    Chapter 16 . . . 95
    My Ten Daily Reminders . . . 94

How Adults with Cancer Can Help Young Loved Ones

    It's Cancer: What Do I Tell My Kids? . . . 99
    Resources . . . 124

About the Contributors

    Patricia P. Gage, Ph.D. . . . 128
    Christopher J. Gage . . . 131
    Marlo Garnsworthy . . . 132

Acknowledgments

So many people have made valuable contribution to the successful completion of this book. To my wonderful family, friends and colleagues who provided support by talking with me about the story, reading parts of the manuscript, offering comments and allowing me to quote their remarks, I will be forever grateful.

I could not have done this book so creatively without Marlo Garnsworthy's expertise as an outstanding editor, writer, illustrator, and writing teacher. She helped edit the story, provided the beautiful prose that made each character and setting come to life, and provided the cover and interior illustrations.

Finally, this book would not have been possible without the loving support of my husband, who has been my inspiration and motivation through all my endeavors for the past thirty-five years. This project has certainly been a blessing and a labor of love.

Introduction

As an engaging and hopeful children's story, *Long Live the Queen* is a tested resource for adults to share with kids when they need to have that difficult discussion about facing cancer. But it is not meant to address issues after someone dies due to cancer. It provides optimism and research-based, proven coping strategies for children and well-tested guidance for parents and other adults who are going through cancer treatment.

Cancer can affect a person's appearance, daily functioning, outlook on life, and ways of interacting and communicating with loved ones. *Long Live the Queen* empowers children to handle such changes by demonstrating positive ways to deal with loss and change from the way things were prior to the diagnosis.

Introduction

Families, as well as teachers and mental health professionals, can use this book to inspire open communication with children who have a loved one with cancer.

My motivation for the book was unleashed right under my nose, literally. After routine monitoring for seasonal allergies, it was recommended by my physician that I have my adenoids removed to get some relief. I was blindsided by a pathology report confirming my dreaded fear: cancer. Although my prognosis was positive, questions began to circulate in my mind as to what to tell colleagues, family, and friends. I learned quickly that adult discussions came rather smoothly, but addressing the questions of children—both my own and those with whom I worked—required some much needed thought.

My son came up with this story when the two of us were on a long road trip, shortly after I finished radiation treatments. While we were discussing how we got through it all as a family, we decided to share what we learned with other families.

Over the years of working on this project, I have invested a lot of time in providing effective coping strategies for the characters in the story, through their dialogue, which you may find useful with your young loved ones as you go through your own journey. The story attempts to take

Introduction

something scary and make it less scary, while empowering kids with things they can do to help their loved one and themselves feel better. My hope is that young readers can relate to the characters and use the same coping skills to deal with what they're going through.

From my own experience, I realized that when a parent or loved one is first diagnosed, there is no time to delve into the literature. *Long Live the Queen*, therefore, features an adult section, which follows the fictional children's story. It offers quick advice and resources using a non-theoretical, short, and to-the-point approach.

In my back-of-the-book recommendations, I was careful to take into account that each family has its own style, religious beliefs, and traditions, as well as emotional makeup. Suggestions are offered regarding what to say and how to handle the information you share with your children. Realize, however, there is no such thing as perfect parenting, or the best way to handle a critical illness like cancer, or only one way to explain it to children. Parents and professionals can expect to make mistakes, as I did along the way.

I suggest that you concentrate on the here and now. Deal with the issues as they come with confidence, and look to the future with hope. Regrets and guilt are a waste of your emotional energy and only serve to paralyze

Introduction

your actions. As you find yourself in the midst of biopsies, possible surgery, radiation, and/or chemotherapy, and trying to somehow manage this new drama in your life, your immediate parental instincts will probably be to shield your children from the frightening reality. Know that you cannot completely protect them, nor is it wise or beneficial in the long run. Accept it as a family affair.

In this book, a fictional story is included that you can use with your young children as a catalyst for discussions. They can be given the story to read on their own, you can read it together, or you can read it to them. Sometimes, it's easier for children to express themselves through the characters of a favorite fairy tale. The characters are given specific things they can do to help, as well as some specific coping skills for how to express and deal with their feelings and questions. The ending was left open-ended and with a sense of optimism, designed for you to tailor it to your specific situation and personal discussion.

Reading to children can also be therapeutic; the story can help children come to grips with an issue that creates emotional turmoil. The book is not meant to take the place of a trained therapist, however, and you do need to keep an open mind.

Remember that, sometimes, it takes more than a thoughtful, caring, and attentive parent to help children through this difficult time.

—Patricia Gage, Ph.D.

Introduction

Long Live the Queen

To the Young Reader

Dear Young Reader,

We are so happy to share with you this story about a very special family who has a loved one with cancer. We hope the story will help take away some of your fears and worries about cancer and its treatments. We also hope it gives you a chance to express your feelings and answer your questions about cancer.

Please don't be afraid to ask questions of the grown-ups you love and trust, no matter how hard it may be, even if you think your questions might make them sad or upset. Remember, there is no such thing as feelings that are right, wrong, good or bad. And there are never feelings that might be so sad you can't share them. Being able to talk about what you think and feel is what will be most helpful to you and everyone in your family.

If you have questions like the ones on the next page, you'll discover the answers in this story.

To the Young Reader

What is cancer?

What's a tumor?

What do the words chemotherapy and radiation mean?

What are side effects?

Is cancer contagious?

Like Isabella in this book, you might be very confused, worried, sad, and even angry sometimes. When a parent or grandparent has cancer, children often feel that way. It's normal. We believe this story will help you understand.

If you know someone being treated for cancer, we encourage you to read this book with a parent or another grown-up. Try some of the things Isabella and her brother do for their mom to help her get through her cancer treatment. There are lots of clever and even fun things you can do. You have an important job in helping your family at a difficult time.

Learning about cancer does not have to be scary for anyone. Scientists and doctors work hard every day to come up with new methods of fighting cancer and different ways to treat it. Think positive and tell yourself, "I'm worried, but I can do it. This will be a tough time for my family, but together we can handle it."

After you read the story, try the "My Ten Daily

Reminders" on page 94. Who knows, some day you may want to share your own ideas to help other children, too.

Hang in there!

—Patricia, Christopher, and Marlo

Long Live the Queen

Chapter 1

A long time ago, in a castle far away, there was a happy princess named Isabella. She lived with her royal family, who brought great joy to the Kingdom of Groveth.

One morning, Princess Isabella and little Prince Phillip skipped through the busy village, waving to the merry townsfolk, all the way to the bustling marketplace.

"Good morning, My Young Majesties," said the grocer, with a hearty smile. "Some fresh peaches for your royal selves?"

Isabella pulled out her purse. "Oh . . . how much will they be?" She had saved her chore money for weeks to buy something special for her mother.

"A gift for the sweet children of King Maximilian and Queen Anna." The grocer beamed as he handed them four fragrant, plump peaches. King Maximilian and Queen Anna were wise, fair, and generous rulers, and the royal family was much loved in the kingdom.

Isabella smiled and thanked the grocer. She spotted exactly what she had been looking for.

Shimmering silk scarves, in more colors than she could imagine, overflowed from the tailor's stall.

"Look, Philip." Isabella pointed to the scarves. "Those purple ones will be perfect for Mummy."

Each night, the king read to Isabella and her little brother. And most nights, before the queen tucked her into bed, Isabella would ask, "Shall we dance the Purple Pajama Polka?"

"Absolutely!" the queen always answered.

Then, together, they'd dance.

Isabella smiled, went straight to the purple silks on the tailor's stall and bought two long, shimmering scarves. One was a bright, rich magenta, the other the bluish hue of violets. The scarves were so light, they wafted on the air as she twirled with them.

As she and Philip climbed the path back to the palace,

Isabella couldn't wait to dance the Purple Pajama Polka that night.

Long Live the Queen

Chapter 2

That evening, Isabella did not wait to be told to take her bath. She had brushed her teeth and hair, and put on her favorite purple pajamas. Now she was ready for bed. Almost.

The magenta and violet scarves were in a package she had carefully tucked beneath her pillow. She could not wait to surprise the queen.

"Have you said your thanks?" asked the king, when he and the queen came to say good night.

Isabella knelt by her bed and listed all the things she was grateful for. ". . . and good health, and Daddy, Mummy and the Purple Pajama Polka . . ." She opened one eye and grinned at her mother. "Shall we dance, Mummy?"

But her mother did not say, "Absolutely!" like she always had before. Instead, she gave a little sigh and said, "Maybe. I'm a little tired tonight."

Isabella frowned. "Oh. That's all right," she said.

The queen looked weary and pale.

Maybe Mummy is getting a cold, Isabella thought. She felt disappointed. The queen had never said no to the Purple Pajama Polka.

"I'm sure I'll feel better by tomorrow," said Queen Anna. "Then we'll do a double super polka to make up for it. And if I'm not feeling better, the village doctor will surely help me."

Princess Isabella thought about her mother's tired face and the pretty scarves under her pillow. She certainly hoped so.

The next morning, the queen was no better. In fact, she seemed a little worse. Her face was still pale and drawn, and now she looked as if she were in pain.

So, after breakfast, the king and queen rode down to the village doctor. They were gone nearly the whole day.

When they finally returned as night fell, her parents were quiet and looked worried.

"Let's all go sit in the playroom," said the king.

"Why have you been gone so long?" asked Prince

Philip. "I thought something bad had happened. I really missed you."

The king hesitated, but with a comforting nod from the queen, he reached out and took their hands.

"We missed you, too," said the queen. "But children, we have a little bad news."

Long Live the Queen

Chapter 3

"The village doctor says your mother is very sick," said the king, and he squeezed the queen's hand. "He says she's stricken with a disease called cancer."

"Cancer?" Isabella frowned. "What's that?" Her parents looked so grave. She hated the sound of the word.

"You know that our bodies are made of cells?" said the king.

Isabella did know that. She had learned it from her governess.

"Cells are the tiny little structures that our bodies are made of," she told Philip, just as the governess had taught her. "They have a very thin skin called a membrane. Our bodies are made up of all kinds of cells. There are muscles cells, blood cells, nerve cells—"

"I don't get it," interrupted Philip, who hadn't yet been taught about cells.

"Well, that's all right," said the queen. "The problem is that some of my cells have changed. They are abnormal. That means they don't act the way they should. Cancer cells don't follow the rules. They make too many new cells when we don't need them. The village doctor found signs of these cells inside my body using special tests. That's why we were gone so long."

"Cancer is when abnormal cells grow and reproduce out of control," said their father.

"Reproduce means they make copies of themselves," Isabella informed Philip.

Philip tilted his head and studied the queen. "But how can you be sick, Mummy? You don't have a fever or spots. When I got sick, I had a fever and spots."

"This cancer is deep on the inside, where you can't see it," said the king. "It is growing as a lump called a tumor. Some tumors are harmless, but some are malignant. That means they're cancerous, and the doctors may have to do a surgery to take them out."

"The village doctor can make you better, can't he?" cried Isabella. "Can't he make the tumor go away? Why do you both look so serious?"

"The doctor said that Mummy's tumor is malignant, but there is nothing he can do to make her better," said the king, sadly. "I'm afraid it is quite serious."

Nobody said it, and Isabella dared not ask, but she thought, *Will Mummy ever get better?*

Instead, she asked, "Why?"

Neither the king nor the queen knew the answer.

Long Live the Queen

Chapter 4

News travels fast in a place like the Kingdom of Groveth. The once happy, bustling village was silenced by the terrible news of the queen's cancer. The people of the kingdom were devastated. They loved Queen Anna, just as they loved wise, fair King Maximilian and the prince and princess.

Even though it was a bright, sunny day, the streets were still, as if a cold, grey fog had swept through town. The children did not run and play, the townsfolk did not joke or gossip, and the few market stalls had closed early.

Isabella felt frightened as she looked to the street below. If the whole town was so sad and worried, her mother's illness must be very serious, indeed.

But King Maximilian had ordered his four fastest knights to search north, east, south, and west.

Isabella watched the villagers salute the brave knights who rode past on their great chargers.

"Surely, someone can treat this terrible illness that is making my beloved queen sick," Isabella heard the king say as his knights galloped away.

"They will be successful," King Maximilian told his children, who watched from the palace balcony. "They simply must be."

As the riders disappeared from sight, Isabella's heart swelled with hope. The four, fine knights would find someone to heal her mother. She just knew it.

That night, after Isabella had brushed her teeth and put on her purple princess pajamas, the queen kissed her good night.

"Good night, Mummy," said Isabella.

"Don't you want to do the Purple Pajama Polka?" The queen stroked Isabella's hair.

"I don't think so," said Isabella. "I think you should rest so you're ready when the knights bring back someone who can help."

"Oh, come on, just a minute or two?" the queen

pleaded. So, together, in their purple pajamas, they danced. Little Philip joined in.

But Isabella's heart wasn't in it. She thought about the purple scarves hidden beneath her pillow. "I think we've danced enough now," she said, after only a minute.

"I feel good," said her mother, hugging Isabella and Philip close. "Don't you worry, my sweet darlings. I'm sure I'll be just fine."

But in the days and weeks that followed, Isabella grew anxious. Her mother didn't look fine. She seemed tired most of the time.

After some days, the knight who had travelled east returned. "I'm sorry, Your Majesty," he told the king, his eyes lowered. "I looked everywhere in the east, but I found no one."

A few days later, the knight who had gone south arrived. Her voice quavered as she said, "I'm sorry, My Liege. I met with many, many doctors, but none can treat this illness."

Only hours later, the knight from the west returned, covered from head to toe in dust. "The western land was treeless and barren, Sire. I could find no one at all."

For a moment, the king hung his head. When he raised it, he looked at Isabella. "We must not lose hope," he said. "There is still the knight who rode north."

Long Live the Queen

Chapter 5

As the days passed, Isabella grew ever more anxious. Nothing seemed very different, and yet nothing seemed quite the same anymore. Isabella still had lessons and chores. The queen seemed fine most of the time. But everyone was waiting.

After a month, the knight from the north had yet to return. Isabella began to lose hope.

One day, she heard a distant sound. Was it the faint clatter of hooves? Isabella ran to the window.

A horse and rider galloped toward the palace. She was certain the small, white speck on the valley road was the knight who had gone north.

The knight leaped from his horse and sprinted into

the castle, breathless and beaming. "Your Highness! I found somebody who can help!" he puffed as he bowed to the king and queen.

The king embraced his loyal knight. "Who is it?"

"A wise wizard," explained the knight. "He lives in the Farnorth Forest."

The Enchanted Forest? thought Isabella. At least, that's what the townsfolk called it.

"We must prepare to leave at once," announced the king. The queen nodded.

"May I go along, Papa?" asked Isabella. "Mummy might be scared. She may need to hold my hand."

The king frowned thoughtfully, and a long look passed between him and his wife.

"I think that would be wonderful," said the queen. "Let's think of this as an adventure."

Within the hour, King Maximilian, Queen Anna and Princess Isabella stepped into their carriage and set off to find the wizard. Isabella waved to Little Philip, who was to stay home with their governess.

Despite the reason for their journey, Isabella couldn't help but feel excited to be going somewhere new. *I mustn't look forward to it,* she scolded herself. It didn't seem right to be excited while her mother was so ill.

For two whole days, they travelled north through mountains and mud, up stony paths and through wide valleys filled with wildflowers. Finally, they reached the edge of Farnorth Forest. They traveled some time beneath the tall, twisted pine trees.

As they neared the wizard's keep, her parents began to sing.

But Isabella didn't feel like singing. She no longer felt excited. As the wizard's keep loomed ahead, she only felt butterflies in her belly.

Long Live the Queen

Chapter 6

Isabella waited with her father while the wizard examined the queen. It took a long, long time, and Isabella grew bored. She thought she might need to jump around the room because, surely, the wizard would make her mother well. Everything could be normal again.

She couldn't sit still any longer. She sat on her hands, crossed her legs, and confined herself to swinging them.

When the wizard finally called them in, he stood stroking his long beard and fidgeting with his hat. In a soft yet powerful voice, he said, "This disease is very serious. But I have a possible remedy for you, a spell that may or may not work. You must be willing to do everything I say to fight this disease."

The king and queen listened closely, their eyes fixed on the wizard. They nodded their agreement.

"There are two steps to this spell," the wizard explained slowly. "First, I will give you a potion. Its name is chemotherapy. It uses different chemicals to get rid of the bad cells."

On the edge of their seats, Isabella and her parents listened carefully.

"The second step is called radiation," the wizard continued. "It's like taking potent energy rays from the sun and using them to zap the tumor. It will destroy the bad cells. For these remedies to work, however, you must return to my Farnorth Forest keep between twenty-five and thirty times."

Isabella looked at her parents' faces. As they held hands, they stared into each other's eyes, then nodded. They seemed so determined and hopeful.

"You must fight with all your might. That means all of you." The wizard looked kindly at the king and Isabella.

What can I do? Isabella wondered to herself. She was beginning to feel scared.

Help for Children Who Have a Loved One With Cancer

Long Live the Queen

Chapter 7

Now filled with hope, the queen, king and Isabella made the long journey home. Isabella thought about all that had happened at the wizard's keep. After the queen took the potion, the wizard had waved his healing wand over her body.

"I must warn you," the wizard had said. "This treatment won't be easy. Chemotherapy and radiation do have side effects that can make you feel tired or nauseous."

Their carriage swayed back and forth, southward down the road, and Isabella said, "How do you feel, Mummy?"

"I'm feeling very hopeful," said the queen.

But by the time their carriage pulled up at the castle, Queen Anna looked pale and tired again, despite her smile.

"Are you better now, Mummy?" Prince Philip asked as he ran out to greet them.

Isabella didn't think so.

"Not yet," said the king. "It is going to take some time."

"Come on, Philip, let's go play in the garden," Isabella said, taking her little brother's hand. "Mummy needs to rest."

Isabella felt very responsible as she tossed a ball to Philip. "We have to be patient. Also, the wizard said the treatment has side effects."

"What's side affex?" asked Philip, catching the ball.

"Side effects means that even though the medicine is helping Mummy, it will also make her quite sick sometimes."

"She's already very sick." Philip frowned. "And medicine is supposed to make you better."

Isabella put her arm around Philip. "The spell's power will make Mummy very tired."

The wizard had also said the queen's hair might start to fall out. As she thought about her mother's beautiful, long hair, Isabella found that impossible to imagine.

Suddenly, her eyes grew wide. "Philip, I have an idea! Let's think of all the ways we can help Mummy around the castle."

"Yay!" said Philip, clapping his little hands.

Soon, they had made a list, and they ran inside to tell the queen.

"I'm going to walk the royal dogs," said Philip, "and I'll set the table for every meal."

"I will help fold the laundry and tend to the royal garden," said Princess Isabella. "And we will both put away our toys and do our homework without being asked more than once."

Her mother looked proud, and Isabella felt happier because now there was something she could do.

But as the weeks passed, and her mother traveled back and forth to the wizard, the treatments sometimes made her very sick, indeed.

Isabella tried to do more and more to help her. She felt frustrated. Even though her mother was resting much more, she didn't seem any better.

Then soon after her mother's fifth visit to the wizard, Isabella noticed something unsettling.

The queen was losing her hair, just as the wizard had predicted. When her mother looked at her reflection in the mirror, she turned away.

Isabella saw tears in her mother's eyes and was frightened.

Long Live the Queen

Chapter 8

The queen's hair had once been long and silky. It had floated and shone as she danced. But her balding head scared Isabella. It seemed strange and ugly, not like her mother at all.

The king asked the royal milliner to make a wig. It was almost the same length and color as her mother's real hair, but it didn't feel the same when Isabella stroked it. It didn't twirl and float when Queen Anna felt well enough to dance.

When Isabella's friends came to play, they couldn't help staring. Her mother looked so strange. And playing games with her friends didn't seem as much fun without her mother joining in or cheering.

Isabella remembered what the wizard had said. The

treatment would be hard, and they all had to work together. To cheer up her mother and raise her spirits, Isabella picked orchids from the garden for her mother's bedside. Some days, she made daisy wreaths for her mother's head or hid cheerful notes for the queen to find.

On days when the queen felt strong enough, she did play with Isabella and Philip. But too often, her illness kept her confined to bed. She felt sick to her stomach and did not say much to anybody. She seemed to wear her pajamas all the time.

One Sunday morning, as Isabella passed the dining room doors, she saw her mother, who was up and smiling and eating a hearty breakfast in her royal purple pajamas.

A feeling of happiness swept through Isabella, and she skipped through the palace halls. Once she began to skip, she couldn't stop.

From its hiding place under her mattress, she took the package with the purple silk scarves and returned to the dining room. She felt as light and floaty as a bubble.

"Purple Pajama Polka?" she asked her mother.

The queen put down her fork and said, "I don't think so, darling." She sighed and explained, saying, "I'm a bit tired right now. As soon as I've eaten breakfast, I'm going to lie back down."

Isabella now felt like a bubble that had popped.

"All right." Isabella's voice was quiet.

Without another word, she left the room and closed the door behind her. She silently made her way to the north tower and climbed to the very top. Once by the highest window, she ripped open the parcel.

"Who needs these stupid, ugly things!" Isabella shouted, and she thrust the delicate, violet-and-magenta silk scarves out through the open window.

They fluttered down and ripped on the thorny rose bushes far below.

Long Live the Queen

Chapter 9

Isabella stamped down the stairs of the north tower. She clomped out of the castle. She stomped through the royal gardens and into the stables.

All of that stamping, clomping, and stomping made her feel a tiny bit better.

She gave a heavy sigh and patted her pony's nose. She told him, "Nibbles, I need to think of good things. Like the times we used to go down to the lake for family picnics. Or our visits to the palace zoo."

Nibbles just listened and nudged her.

It didn't help. These days, her mother never had the energy to visit the royal zoo or go on picnics.

Soon, Isabella was even madder.

"It just isn't fair!" she shouted, then she wailed.

Nibbles snorted and stepped away.

Just then, she heard footsteps behind her. Her father was leading his horse into the stable.

"You sound a little mad," he said.

Isabella just folded her arms and leaned against her pony's warm side.

"When you were little and you felt mad, you went to your swing under the great yew tree," said the king. "Do you remember? You swung back and forth until you felt much better."

Isabella did remember. "I swung all afternoon when I didn't get that white pony I wanted," she said. "But that was stupid!" She wiped an angry tear from her cheek.

The king was quiet for a moment.

"Sometimes, when you were really, really mad, you sat in your room and scribbled," he said. "You drew the reason you were mad. Then you stomped to the top of the north tower and tossed it out the window."

Isabella gave a weak smile and felt her face turning bright pink. It seemed that littering from the north tower window had always been a bad habit.

"Afterward, though, you always felt better very quickly."

The king chuckled. "You saw your worries and anger float away on the breeze."

"One day, I drew a picture of you with fangs and crossed eyes," Isabella said and snickered.

"I know!" the king said and snorted. "Mummy found it while she was gardening. Oh, we had a good old laugh. I kept it, you know. It reminds me to keep a smile on my face." He gently tapped the tip of her nose and grinned.

"I wonder if scribbling would make me feel better now?" said Isabella.

"It might," said the king.

Isabella sighed. "I will try hard to feel better."

"You always try hard. I know that, and Mummy knows that, too. And we're both very thankful and proud of you."

As Isabella hugged him, she had a new idea.

Long Live the Queen

Chapter 10

If Mummy can't play with us, thought Isabella, *we will bring the fun to her.*

So, when the queen felt well enough, Isabella read to her. She, Philip, and the queen played board games as they sat on the queen's giant bed. Sometimes, they put on little plays for her to watch.

Other days, though, Isabella found the queen lying in bed without her wig. She looked very pale. And on those days, she didn't ask her mother to play. She just lay beside her and held the queen's hand or cuddled her.

One morning, Prince Philip looked pale, too. "I have a sore throat," he said and started to cough. "Mummy, can I hop into bed with you?"

"Sorry, my sweet boy," the queen said softly. "I'm unable to take care of you right now. I have to stay away from anyone who is sick. My body needs all its energy to fight the bad cancer cells. If I get a cold, too, my body will have to work twice as hard."

"But who will take care of me?" Philip looked scared and backed away.

The queen sweetly said, "All I want is to hug you, make your favorite tomato soup, and read you a story until you fall asleep. I just want to make you feel better. Until I am well, however, your father will take care of you if you're sick. We can blow kisses to each other, and Papa will give you lots of hugs."

"I'll take care of you, too, Philip," said Isabella, patting his arm.

Philip slipped his hand into hers. He looked so sad and sneezy.

That night, after lights out, Philip knocked on Isabella's bedroom door.

"What's the matter, Phillykins?" said Isabella. "Can't you sleep?"

"No." Philip sat down on her bed and hugged his teddy tightly. "I have a runny nose."

"I know," she said, "but you'll be better soon."

"But Bella," croaked Philip, his eyes wide and serious, "I haven't got spots or a fever, just like Mummy. Maybe I don't have a cold. Maybe I caught cancer, like Mummy."

Isabella didn't think they could catch cancer from the queen, but she really wasn't sure.

"What if I got it from Mummy when I last hugged her?" whispered Philip, who now looked very frightened.

Isabella didn't know what to say. What if Philip had caught cancer? And what if she caught it, too?

She went to the window and stared out. Far below, the scarves fluttered in the rosebushes, their purples dark and murky in the moonlight.

"Let's go and talk to Papa and Mummy," she finally said.

"I don't want to upset Mummy," sniffed Philip. "I don't want to make her feel worse."

Isabella took Philip's hand. "C'mon on, Phillykins. You'll be all right. You'll see."

She led him to the palace parlor where her parents both read by the fire. When she explained their worries, the queen gave a gasp.

"Oh, no, my darlings, I hadn't realized we didn't talk about that. I'm so sorry you've been worried."

"No, my dears," said the king. "Cancer is not contagious, like chickenpox or a cold."

"Not contagious means you can't catch it," Isabella told Philip. She couldn't help but laugh with relief.

"You can always talk to us if you want to know more or when you're worried," said the king. "I'm so glad you weren't afraid to ask us about it."

"Well, I was afraid at first, but Isabella was really brave." Philip stood up straight and tall. "So, I got really brave, too!"

"You sure did," said Isabella. But she knew she wasn't always brave.

One time, when the queen cried, Isabella began to cry, too. She tried to hide it so her mother wouldn't see, but she did see. Of course, her mother somehow always knew when her children were upset. And somehow, she always understood. Isabella loved that about her.

"When grown-ups feel hurt, sad, or scared," the queen explained tenderly, "they may cry, just as children do. It's all right to cry, and it's all right to ask questions when you don't understand something. It is important to talk about your thoughts and feelings with people who love you."

Isabella felt much better about that. She knew she could talk to her mother about anything—except, perhaps, for one thing.

Help for Children Who Have a Loved One With Cancer

Long Live the Queen

Chapter 11

One day, the queen looked well. "Let's go down to the market," she said. "I so miss seeing the townsfolk."

Isabella and Philip were excited. They got ready, and the queen put on a colorful dress and her crown.

"Mummy, aren't you going to wear your wig, too?" asked Isabella.

Sometimes, her mother wore a hat or crown alone, but it didn't disguise her baldness.

Isabella looked away as her mother took off the crown. And when she looked back, her mother was wearing both, just as Isabella had wanted.

The queen's face looked tight, as if her feelings were

hurt, but she brightened as they went around in the village. It felt just like old, happier times.

On the way home from the market, they stopped by the lake.

"You know, sometimes, when I feel sad or mad, I think about doing this." The queen took two large leaves from the ground, curled them around, and put a twig through them so it looked like a boat. She whispered a wish into it and placed it on the water's surface.

Together, they watched the little leaf boat float away.

"As you watch your creation disappear across the lake, you can feel your sadness and anger drift away. Would you like to try it?"

"But I don't feel sad or angry," said Isabella. "I feel wonderful."

"That's great!" said her mother. She gave Isabella a squeeze. "It can also be helpful if you end each day by writing in your journal about something you're grateful or happy for. That's what I do. It isn't too hard to think of wonderful things, especially when I have you two."

"I'm grateful for today," said Isabella. It had been almost perfect. Maybe they could even do the polka together tonight.

"I'm grateful for boats!" Prince Philip yelled from the lake shore.

While Philip played with his boats, the queen sat down next to Isabella on the grass.

"I know it's been especially hard for you to see me lose my hair," she said quietly.

Isabella felt her face flush red. She did not want to talk about the queen's baldness. It made her uncomfortable and confused.

"You don't have to be afraid to touch my head or worry that I'm going to look bad," said the queen. "You certainly don't have to be embarrassed when people see me bald."

"I'm not ashamed of you," Isabella said at last, but she knew her mother's baldness did embarrass her.

"I've noticed you often remind me to wear my wig," said the queen.

"It makes you look more normal," said Isabella, who tugged at the grass.

"If it bothers you, just say to yourself, 'This is only for a short time. Mummy will get her beautiful hair back.'"

That just didn't seem possible to Isabella. Uncle Prince Albert had been balding since she had known him, and now his head was as slick and shiny as a hard-boiled egg. His hair never grew back. Maybe Mummy was wrong. What if she were bald ... forever?

She remembered how her mother's long hair had twirled around her as they danced. It seemed the Purple Pajama Polka would never be the same again.

Help for Children Who Have a Loved One With Cancer

Long Live the Queen

Chapter 12

By autumn, the time had come for the wizard to check on his spell's progress. Early one dark, chilly morning, Isabella stood on the palace balcony. Below, Queen Anna and King Maximilian bundled up in the royal carriage and began the long journey north.

It was so hard waiting four days for the news. Each day, Isabella felt her heart beat a little faster. Her stomach hurt, and she felt anxious. She tried all the things that often helped her feel calmer or that brightened her spirits.

The king had said that when she felt nervous and upset, she should take deep, slow breaths. Belly breaths, he called them. That often made her feel better. But today, the slow and deep belly breaths didn't seem to be working.

"Papa said we can also count backward from twenty. That might distract us from thinking about things that worry and upset us," Isabella told Philip.

"Twenty, eleven, three, two, one!" yelled Philip, who jumped around like a carnival jester.

He wasn't listening to Isabella, and she was annoyed.

"How can you be silly at a time like this?" she snapped.

Philip looked so hurt, Isabella instantly felt bad. "Let's try thinking of something that really makes us feel good."

Just as Isabella thought of the Purple Pajama Polka, the royal carriage appeared over the horizon. She took Philip's hand and led him to their playroom to wait for their parents.

The news was not good.

When he came to the playroom, the king told his children, "The wizard said the tumor is not shrinking. The spell does not seem to be working."

"I feel like it's never going to end!" Isabella cried out. She was wringing her hands.

"I wish things could be as easy as they were before the cancer," said her father. "It's all right to feel sad or even get mad. It's how you handle it that matters."

"I'm sick of it, and I hate it," said Isabella.

There was no one who could help her. When the

villagers needed help, they came to see the king and queen. They explained their problem or idea, and the king and queen always had a solution. But there was nothing they could do about this problem, and that made Isabella mad.

Long Live the Queen

Chapter 13

Isabella ran out of the throne room. The pounding of her footsteps echoed through the castle's stone halls and down the steps. She didn't stop running until she'd reached the lake. Unable to catch her breath, she laid her head on a stone and cried in great, gulping sobs.

In her mind, she heard her father's voice say, "Take slow, deep breaths. Think of things that make you happy."

But what can I think of? Isabella wondered. So many of her happy memories were of her mother.

Even this spot by the lake was where they always had their picnics together. Her mother loved to watch the ducks and thought they were silly and funny. But now there was ice on the lake, and most of the ducks had flown south for the winter. The world seemed bleak and hopeless.

"I can't think of anything that makes me feel good! I'm not happy!" Isabella shouted, and she wiped her tears on her sleeve. "I feel like I won't ever be happy again!"

As she said it, Isabella wasn't sure she meant it. But what if it were true? What if they were never to be happy again? It was a miserable thought.

She remembered what the wizard had said, that all of them had to work hard. Isabella had tried hard. She had done extra chores and learned new ways to help. She sat on the leaf-strewn lawn, gazing at the cold lake. She thought about the last time she was here with the queen.

Isabella picked up a large leaf, twisted it, and shoved a twig through it.

She spoke into the little wish-boat. "I wish things could be the way they were." But in her mind she knew it was an impossible wish.

She set the little wish-boat on the water. It skimmed over a grey wave and quickly sank.

So, she tried again.

"I wish cancer would disappear forever!" She shouted her words into the wish-boat this time, and she thrust it onto the lake.

The few remaining ducks paddled busily in the icy water. One of them spotted the boat and tried to gobble it. The other ducks quacked and splashed, trying to steal it.

"Hey, stop that, ducks!" Isabella tried not to giggle, but she simply couldn't help it. The ducks were funny. "Well, that's one way to get rid of something."

Her mother would have thought that was funny, too. Isabella remembered that Uncle Albert always said it was healthy to laugh. So, maybe making her mother laugh would help her.

She curled up another leaf, gently pierced it with a twig, and whispered, "I wish to laugh more." But then she took it back. She knew what to say now. It suddenly seemed very clear.

"I wish for Mummy to feel joy," she whispered into the wish-boat.

As it floated across the surface, the boat twirled in a patch of twinkling, bright sunlight before racing across the water. When it was gone from view, Isabella smiled and headed for the castle.

As she neared the north tower, something caught her eye. The violet and magenta scarves were tattered now and were tangled in the rosebushes where they'd landed months before. But their little frayed edges drifted prettily in the breeze, as soft and gently flowing as her mother's hair had been.

A sudden smile stole across Isabella's face. She had an amazing idea.

Help for Children Who Have a Loved One With Cancer

Long Live the Queen

Chapter 14

One week later, Isabella bounded into her mother's bedchamber. The queen was in front of her mirror, gazing at her reflection. Her hair sat in sad, thin tufts on her now nearly bald head. When she saw Isabella, she turned away, grabbed the wig from her dressing table and quickly tugged it on.

Isabella saw tears in her mother's eyes, and for a just a moment, her throat felt tight. But she swallowed hard, took a deep belly breath, and smiled.

"What is it, my sweetness?" the queen said.

"I have something for you." Isabella held out a package. "And I'm going to give it to you right now."

"How lovely." The queen's eyes brightened.

"There's one important condition," said Isabella. "You'll have to take off that wig."

Her mother hesitated, but Isabella's wide grin made her mother smile broadly, too.

"All right, then. I shall." The queen peeled off the wig and dropped it onto the dressing table. Still smiling, she took the parcel Isabella offered her.

Isabella held her breath. All week, she had risen before dawn to work on the gift. She'd given up her playtime. She had not even been to ride Nibbles. It had been hard work and tricky, but at last her gift was complete.

The queen's eyes were wide with wonder as she lifted out the twig-and-leaf crown Isabella had woven with the wispy, frayed silk scarves. The magenta and violet colors had faded in the rain and sun but were still soft and pretty. They brought a colorful glow to her mother's face as she placed it upon her head.

"It's beautiful, Isabella." The queen admired Isabella's gift in the mirror.

"You are beautiful in it," said Isabella, still smiling. "And it will keep your head warm now that the weather's getting cooler. No more need for silly wigs."

"Thank you, darling," said her mother. "This crown is

fit for a queen."

Isabella told her mother about the ducks and what had happened to her wish-boat. They both laughed so hard they cried. Isabella spoke about the wish-boat that had danced in the sunlight.

"Then," said Isabella, "I saw the scarves. And I knew how to make my wish come true!"

"Let's go out," said the queen. "I want to see these ducks. They need to see my crown, too."

Her mother looked happy as she watched Isabella and Philip play on the lake shore. Her cheeks were pink, and she had a sparkle in her eyes.

"Now she just needs somewhere really special to wear her crown," Isabella told Philip.

Philip nodded. "Like a party," he said. "It's a very good crown for a party."

"A really big party," said Isabella, "where she can see how much everybody loves her."

"And how grateful we are to have her," added Philip.

"Let's talk to Papa." Isabella winked at Philip.

Long Live the Queen

Chapter 15

It was Sunday morning, and Isabella was excited. She and Philip hid in the grand dining room.

They heard their mother calling, "Isabella? Phillip? Aren't you coming to breakfast? Ethel, my dear, where is everyone?" they heard her ask a maid. "Have you seen the prince and princess, or the king? It seems as if the castle is almost deserted."

"I don't know about everyone, Your Highness," said Ethel, "but I believe Your Majesty's meal is waiting for you in the royal dining room. Perhaps the children are there."

The queen thanked Ethel.

Isabella saw Ethel wink toward the dining room as the queen turned away.

Her mother seemed to have more energy today, and her footsteps tapped quickly along the hallway. As she now did every day, she wore the special crown Isabella had made her.

Wide-eyed and smiling, Isabella nudged Philip. "She's coming," she whispered. Isabella's purple silk pajamas rustled loudly as she smoothed them down.

"Shhh, Isabella's jammies!" Philip scolded. He wore purple pajamas, too. "You're going to give us away!"

As their mother entered the dining room, she smiled. "I wondered where you two were." She looked at them in surprise. "Why are you still in your pajamas?" she asked. "What are you up to?"

Isabella noticed her mother's eyes were glowing in a way she hadn't seen in some time.

Philip held up a silk blindfold. "If you want to know, you'll have to put this on."

The queen laughed with delight. "All right..."

Isabella then slipped her hand into her mother's and gently tugged her to the double doors of the palace balcony. Philip quietly opened the doors, and Isabella led her out.

"Now, bend over," Philip told his mother.

She bent down, and he pulled off the blindfold.

The queen gasped when she stood.

The courtyard below was full of jugglers on unicycles, jesters prancing in circles, and ponies shaking their manes and tails. Musicians played and sang the queen's favorite song. The townsfolk smiled and waved up to the queen. King Maximilian and Uncle Albert danced a jig and tipped their hats to Queen Anna.

And every single person was wearing pajamas.

"What is this festival for?" asked the bewildered queen.

"It's a gigantic pajama party, Mummy, and it's all for you!" said Isabella.

Long Live the Queen

Chapter 16

Princess Isabella, Prince Philip, and the queen ran together down to the courtyard, where the king and so many people from her beloved kingdom greeted her lovingly.

The local grocer proudly handed the queen baskets of the freshest fruits and vegetables, and he gave her a jug of fresh milk from his cows. The local librarian brought the queen's favorite story scrolls for the prince and princess to read to her. The tailor presented her with a fine new pair of silk pajamas, woven in many shades of purple. The local puppeteers put on a funny puppet show and promised to return every month until the queen felt better.

Long Live the Queen

The most special gift was from Princess Isabella and Prince Philip. They had made her a book. On each page was a coupon that the queen could redeem at any time. There were coupons for hugs and kisses, coupons for massages for her feet, neck, and back, coupons for special walks together, for playing her favorite music, and for a special delivery of warm milk and cookies.

After a little while, Isabella could see her mother was getting tired.

Isabella led the queen back to her bedchamber and out onto the balcony. When the crowd below saw them, they roared with good cheer and began to wave and smile once more.

Isabella slid her hand into her mother's, and they waved back to the people below them.

"Long live the queen!" the crowd chanted, and then louder, "Long live THE QUEEN!" Again, and even louder, "LONG LIVE THE QUEEN!"

Her mother's face glowed, and her eyes shone. She seemed radiant and filled with joy.

At that moment, Isabella knew nothing could stand in the way of Queen Anna's recovery, and she could see her mother knew it, too.

The queen looked at Isabella and said, "Shall we dance the Purple Pajama Polka?"

"Absolutely!" said Isabella.

Before the cheering crowd below, and while wearing their royal, purple pajamas and their crowns, the queen and Isabella danced the most joyful Purple Pajama Polka they'd ever danced.

The End

My Ten Daily Reminders

1. I will spend time with my mom/dad every day and let them know how much I love them.

2. I will be more patient when the grown-ups around me seem cranky and sad.

3. I will do more things for myself, such as keeping my room clean, putting my stuff away and doing my homework, without being asked.

4. I'll be quiet when I'm in the house, in case my mom or dad need to rest.

5. When I'm sad or mad, I will talk to a grown-up I trust. I will not keep my feelings a secret, and I'll never be afraid to cry or show my feelings.

6. I'll remember that if adults are busy and can't play or spend time with me, it's not because they don't love me. Dealing with cancer is hard on everyone.

7. When I start to worry or feel sad or mad, I will take deep, slow, belly breaths and think about something that makes me happy.

8. I will leave happy and cheerful sticky notes for members of my family, and I will share jokes to make them smile and laugh more often.

9. If I have a cold or feel sick, I will throw kisses to my mom/dad and go to other grown-ups I trust for hugs.

10. I will keep a daily journal by my bed and write down one thing that I'm grateful for each day before I go to sleep.

Long Live the Queen

How Adults with Cancer Can Help Young Loved Ones

It's Cancer: What Do I Tell My Kids?

You have been diagnosed with cancer. You are filled with every conceivable emotion and have a million questions, but the one you ask yourself constantly is, "Why me?" Your heart tells you to shield your loved ones from your pain, but the reality is that you cannot protect them; you will actually need their help to fight this unwelcome giant that has invaded your life. You have to find the words to explain your diagnosis to your children and help them cope with it.

Before you decide what you're going to say and to whom you are going to say it, first, you must deal with your own fears and anxieties. It is important to find ways to release your anger. Allow an appropriate amount of time to deal with your grief. Answer your own questions before you tackle the questions and concerns of your children or loved ones. Once you become informed about your disease and determine your treatment plan, you will then be ready to help your children in a positive way.

What do I say to my children?

Commit to being truthful with your children. If you choose to exclude details of your disease, it allows their own logic and imagination to take over. This may be far more dramatic than the reality of your situation. And by avoiding use of the word *cancer*, you send a message that you have something *so* awful that you can't even say it.

Furthermore, older kids can feel unimportant and confused when they're not included in the conversation and may feel they're not trusted with important family issues. This approach only contributes to mistrust and can invite possible maladaptive coping mechanisms that may be detrimental to your child's emotional well-being in the long run.

Open communication is the best defense against inaccurate information. Tell them the type of cancer you have, the events leading to its discovery, where the cancer is in your body, and what will happen during treatment. Let them know the cancer was discovered in your body before it had a chance to make you really sick—if that is the case—and that is good news.

By guiding the information, communicating directly with your children, engaging them in conversation, and encouraging them to ask questions and express their emotions, whatever they may be, you will be helping them cultivate more positive coping skills. Remember, you are not only helping your child cope with your illness, you are also setting a foundation of trust and connectedness that will help them handle difficult emotions and challenging times throughout their lives.

How should I tell them?

Speaking with your children will be difficult. Prepare and practice what you want to say for that first conversation. Choose a familiar, quiet, and comfortable place. When you're ready to have the discussion with your children, it's best if both parents can do it together. If that's not possible, ask another trusted family member to be with you.

Before you start, you might want to prepare them for the possibility that you might feel sad or get upset during your conversation. If you feel like crying, pause, take some slow deep breaths, and keep going. You won't be hurting them if they see you cry a little, and you're modeling how they can have strong feelings but can learn to handle them.

Let your children know that they can come to you with any questions and can expect that you will tell them the truth. Schedule family meetings often, and encourage them to share their thoughts and feelings, while they find out about your progress and any new information.

Reassure your children that, together, the family will get through this difficult time, and set some family fun time together.

Consider your child's developmental age

While encouraging truthfulness, how much detail you give and how much technical information you share with your children should be dependent on your children's age and maturity level. If you have children of different ages, you may want to have the conversation with your older children first, and have the discussion with the others shortly after. That way, all members hear it from you and have a chance to discuss it further together and support each other.

While the age ranges provided below can serve as a general guide, keep in mind that each child is unique, and they all develop at their own pace. You, as the parent, can be the best judge of how much information about your illness you should share with your child. You may feel you're saying the same things in different ways as you consider their intellectual capabilities, their age, their maturity levels and how they have handled difficult situations in the past (such as moving, starting a new school, the loss of a loved one). If you use their questions as a guide, you'll be giving them what they're able to handle. Children tend to come back with more questions when they're ready for more information.

Ages 0 to 3

If you have babies and children below the age of three, the best thing you can do is keep them near you as much as possible, or have a familiar, trusted adult—one who is a consistent part of your children's lives—spend time with them daily. If your child has a transitional object, such as a blanket or stuffed animal, make sure the caregivers know so the child has it available at all times. A blanket with your scent will be even better. Also have the relative or baby-sitter maintain the baby's routine and continue to maintain the same limits you set before you became ill.

Set up frequent visits to the hospital, hug them, and play with them as much as possible. Since the baby is used to your voice, plan for time when you must be apart by recording some familiar lullabies and reassuring words saying you will see him soon.

Keep in mind that infants are only aware of what is immediately available in front of them. They can only focus on what they see, hear, touch, and their physical interactions with their environment. They enjoy and benefit from rituals and stories. Answer toddlers' questions simply, even if it is the same question over and over again.

Ages 4 to 7

Give simple explanations that Mommy or Daddy is sick, and that the doctors are helping make them better. Reassure them that if you look sad or tired, it's because of your cancer and not because of something they did. They did not make you sick.

For this age group, you will need to be prepared to address their need for more reassurance, which can be brought out by your absence and separation. They will need frequent reminders that they will always be cared for. Make sure their caregivers stick to their daily routine. Give them something special of yours to carry or wear, such as a piece of jewelry, and tell them that when they start to miss you, they can look at this special gift and be reminded of how much you love them—even though you are apart for a little while, you always carry them in your heart.

Children in this age group often do not have the emotional development and insight to express their real feelings or label them with words. They tend to express their feelings through play, drawings, or through stories that cover the subject matter. You will be able to monitor how well they're dealing with the situation by monitoring their moods on a daily basis and how they react to day-to-day situations. If they're quick to anger, seem cranky, sad, overly sensitive, or over-reactive to minor situations, they may need more one-on-one time and reassurance.

If you get briefly emotional when you're talking about your cancer to this age group, it's okay, but if you are overly reactive and emotional over a prolonged period of time, you can actually frighten them and make them more anxious. But if you both start to cry during these conversations, reassure them that it's sometimes fine to cry. Don't be surprised if they quickly change the subject and want to go off to play and continue their activities. When they want to know more, they'll come back with more questions.

Children in this age group enjoy using their imagination, and they are able to learn that their behavior has consequences and effects on others. They also begin to ask questions besides why, how, and when, but they can be easily confused by change. Keep instructions clear and simple and, once again, stick to their daily routine.

Ages 8 to 13

Children ages eight to thirteen are much more imaginative and have more developed concrete thinking and reasoning skills. By the time they are around eleven years old, they are able to think about multiple variables in a systematic way, formulate hypotheses, and consider multiple possibilities. If you are not straightforward with the details, they will start to formulate their own explanations, and this may add more complications to addressing their concerns.

They need to be told about your illness and be kept up to date about your treatment. Reassure them that they did not cause the cancer and that it's not contagious. Be prepared to answer their questions honestly, including, "Are you going to die?" Be as truthful as possible without giving too much detail. You can say, "Some people do die from cancer, but right now my doctors are treating the part of my body where they found the cancer so they can stop the cancer and get rid of it. If anything changes, we will let you know."

Encourage them to ask questions and express feelings, even if they think it's going to upset you. However, if they don't want to talk about their feelings, accept it and don't pressure them to do so.

If the hospital offers a support group, try to get them to join. Encourage them to write you notes, make drawings, and send you text and voice messages as a way of staying closely connected. Arrange for your children to participate in after school activities so they stay busy, and make sure they don't feel bad about having fun with their friends. Sometimes, kids worry so much about their parents' cancer that they want to stay home to make sure nothing happens to the ill parent. It's important to convey that they need to go to school and work hard, just like you are working hard to fight this terrible disease and get well. Validate their concerns, show how much you appreciate their caring way, and set a special time that you can spend together after school or as soon as possible. This will help you both have something to look forward to.

Teens need a different type of support

Teenagers are the toughest group to address because their responses can be highly unpredictable. Teens can fluctuate between being mature and responsible to regressing and becoming very childlike in their behaviors. On the one hand, you may try to protect them because you think they're not mature enough to handle this, but you may also want to prepare them to cope with adversities they may face in the future.

Provide detailed information about your diagnosis, such as the name of the cancer, its symptoms, and possible side effects of the treatment, if you're going to have surgery, what they may expect as a result of your treatment, such as hair loss and fatigue, and anything else that may be relevant.

Since they struggle with their need to be independent, they may feel uncomfortable expressing their feelings in front of you, to avoid upsetting you or appearing weak. Instead, they may become distant and choose to talk to their friends. They may also keep to themselves and pretend they can deal with it on their own, when they actually might be feeling very sad and alone. You, or someone else you trust, need to monitor them to make sure they are not becoming more anxious, moody, depressed, or quick to anger. Check on their school performance to make sure they are keeping up with their work and that their performance is consistent.

Keep reminding them that their feelings may be difficult to talk about and their behavior at times difficult to explain, yet it's expected and normal. Provide suggestions for appropriate outlets to express their thoughts and feelings, such as journaling, writing, music, drawing, and other creative and dramatic arts. Also, encourage participation in athletics, which provides an opportunity to dissipate frustration and anger, and may create an endorphin-induced sense of well-being.

It's important to respect their need for privacy and to encourage them to talk to a professional they can trust at school or at the hospital where you are receiving your treatment. Ask them if they would also like to have their teachers check in with them daily. Some teenagers like that kind of attention, while others don't want to have their teachers ask them about it daily.

Some may want to be involved in your treatments by going with you. Give them the opportunity to come, and encourage them to ask your doctors and nurses any questions they may have. They may also show an interest in helping with chores at home. It's important to let them feel like they are involved, have some control over the situation and can be helpful to you. Just make sure you don't overburden them; allow them to still be children. Remind them often how important it is to you that they're still having fun and spending time with friends, and that they certainly should not feel bad or guilty about it. Teens should also be given the option to choose the people with whom they want to stay after school when their parents can't be there.

Share your emotions

Sharing your emotions is appropriate, acceptable, and certainly expected. You are modeling for your children through this difficult time, and it is okay for all of you to show emotion. You may find yourself saying something like, "I'm crying because I'm feeling sad that I'm sick."

If, every time you try to talk to your children, regardless of their age, you get upset and can't seem to find the words, don't sweat it. Take some slow, deep breaths, relax and ask an expert to help you. Encourage your children to talk to someone other than you, ideally, a person with whom they feel close and can trust with their feelings. This is particularly important for your teenagers. Set up a meeting with your oncology nurse, who is usually well versed in helping patients learn how to talk to their children about what they are facing.

Accept your children's feelings and ways of coping

It is acceptable for your children to experience all kinds of feelings, negative or positive. Keep in mind that some children may not demonstrate much concern or seem sympathetic about your illness. Some may actually resent the interference with their usual, daily life, and they may appear frustrated, instead of caring. Accept it. Remind yourself that children can be self-absorbed. They may actually need a lot more reassurance that their needs will be taken care of, that you'll try hard to maintain their routine and minimize changes in their lifestyle, and that you love them, even if you're not going to be there to tell them as often.

Don't be surprised if they have difficulty identifying and labeling their feelings. They may cry or seem agitated and may not be able to name what they feel. You may need to help them identify and label their emotions. If they cry, let them know it's okay. Tears are a healthy way to wash away hurt, anger or frustration. Tell them you cry, too. If children ask questions and show the need for clarification, listen to their words and feelings, and respond to their questions using real terms, repeating information as needed.

Maintain consistent and predictable routines and limits

It is also important to maintain children's routines within their familiar surroundings. Try to maintain your child's mealtimes and other activities, and avoid changes as much as possible. Even if people from outside your home come to help you, ask them to follow these routines.

Prepare your children for times when changes in their routine will occur, and help them anticipate how their lives will change. Make an effort to alert your children to any upcoming changes, and ask for their input about what they would like to happen. This also gives them a little sense of control.

Like routines, limits provide predictability and help kids feel safer. It's certainly not a good time to ease up on family rules and expectations about homework, chores, curfews, etc. Maintain a balance between asking children to help out with chores without too much disruption to their daily routine, while also allowing them to be children.

Remember, above all, children need to feel confident that they will always have food, shelter, and plenty of love. Make every effort to notice how your children are coping, and reinforce their efforts.

Monitor behavioral changes

Children respond with different types of emotional, physical, and cognitive reactions to stressful events. Their reactions to previous life experiences, their support systems, and the level of attachment to the individual going through the critical illness all play a significant role in how they will handle the situation.

Look for changes in your children's behavior and mood. The regressive behaviors listed below are some of the symptoms children may display as a response to a parent's illness.

- a school age child suddenly being afraid to

spend the night at a friend's house,
- being unable to sleep without a comfort object that has been put away for quite some time,
- excessive clinging to the parent going through the illness,
- decrease or increase in appetite,
- sleeplessness,
- stomachaches,
- headaches,
- agitation,
- loss of interest in usual activities,
- difficulty concentrating,
- crying often,
- reporting feeling sad a lot,
- choosing to spend a lot of time alone,
- school grades dropping,
- excessive outbursts of anger, and
- getting in trouble in school for disturbing the class

You can try to engage your child in conversation about the particular behavior by saying, "I know my cancer has been hard on all of us, but we need to try to help each other," or "I noticed that you got really mad at your sister over XYZ. Do you want to talk about it?" or

"How can I help?"

Normally, there should be a gradual decrease in these symptoms over time. If parents monitor their children's emotional reactions closely and act quickly to help them develop more positive coping responses during the time of the illness, they can regain equilibrium and not allow it to affect their day-to-day functioning. But if the frequency and severity increases, referral to a mental health professional may be necessary. Building your children's confidence and resilience in handling difficult times is the best gift you can give them.

Inform your children's school

You may want to check with your child's school to see if a guidance counselor or school psychologist is available for your child to talk to. Ask counselors and teachers to closely monitor your children's class work, behavior, and mood. It's important to let your child know that you are letting his teachers know about your illness and ask for their help.

Some kids want to keep things private and may prefer not to talk about it in school or with their friends. Encourage them to reach out to people who care about them and are invested in their well-being, but involve them in that decision.

You may want to consider ongoing counseling for your child as you go through your treatments. Your local hospital may also have a program or support group for kids that provides education and counseling. Some schools offer the Rainbows program in small groups, which has been highly successful for children going through significant changes in their families due to loss, illness, or divorce.

If you begin to feel that you are not being a good parent, or you find yourself too weak or emotional to deal with your children's needs and emotional concerns by yourself, it's important and necessary to include experts to help you reassure yourself often that you're doing what's best for your child and that you are meeting their needs first.

What to tell others

Families differ in how much information they are willing to share with others about their illness. In making this decision, try to keep your child's life as normal as possible. Help them prepare their response for when people ask them about their mom or dad's cancer. If they feel like answering a particular question, they should. If asked a question they don't want to answer, they can politely say, "Thanks for asking, but you might want to ask my mom or dad about that."

Dealing with cancer and the effects of radiation, chemotherapy, and surgery will make it hard to maintain secrecy. It will be almost impossible to act as if the illness is inconsequential. You cannot hide or control the possible unexpected problems or scares during your treatment and recovery process. Changes such as hair loss, fatigue, vomiting, frequent headaches, weight loss, and extended travel to other cities to visit specialists for treatment are to be expected.

During my own battle with this dreaded disease, within three weeks of beginning radiation treatments, due to suppressed activity in my salivary glands, I began to experience severe dryness of my mouth and throat, which made it difficult to eat or swallow without fluids. I also suffered from a loss of appetite, fatigue, loss of smell, loss of taste, loss of hair on the back of my head, as well as a significant hearing loss. I was left with visible burns, skin dryness and discoloration of my face and around my neck, which remain noticeable but are no longer painful. The good news is that many side effects may gradually go away, just as the painful experiences may gradually fade from your memory.

Allow others to help

No one can handle it all. Allow people to help you,

and accept it graciously. Allow your friends and family to help with errands or driving your children to their various activities. In fact, you may want to have a close friend or family member, trusted by your child, to coordinate help from others and well-wishers.

Your friends and loved ones can be helpful without being intrusive or disturbing your precious family time. You need time to rest. You need alone time with your spouse and close friends to refuel and get the emotional support you need. Let them spoil you. It makes them feel good to do something to help you. You need the attention, the pampering and the time to share what is happening to you.

Take an active role

From the moment you receive your diagnosis, and throughout your course of treatment, you must be willing to take an active role in your treatment options and to determine how you are going to interact and communicate with your loved ones about your illness.

Pursue your treatment and recovery as you would a job you value. Take it very seriously. Work at it effectively. Believe that many people are relying on you to get the job done and get well. Make informed decisions concerning your choice of doctors and treatment options.

Your wellness involves your body, mind and spirit. Seeking harmony between all three is crucial. Develop a regimen for which you schedule what you need to do to stay healthy as part of your work day. If they value what you do for the organization, people who work with you will understand how important this plan is to you. Consult with a nutritionist to make sure you are getting the appropriate nutrients that cancer can deplete from your body. Exercise daily to regain your vitality and muscle strength. If you need time to rest, give yourself permission to do just that. Your well-being has to become the highest priority in your life.

Staying healthy and emotionally connected with people you care about should become your personal quest in life. You need to be around healthy people doing normal things and stay as active as possible. Avoid feeling like a victim held hostage by the cancer. This can only bring you down to a state of powerlessness, which can make you useless to your children.

When I planned my course of treatment, since it was out of town, my husband and I decided it would be best if I stayed at a medical hotel near the hospital so I didn't have far to travel. If anything happened to me, I could easily be admitted to the hospital. Within a week of this arrangement, I began to get depressed and anxious about the possible outcome of my cancer. Wherever I went, I saw people walking around with IVs, without hair, with bandages and scars, looking weak and pale. I could not relate to any of them. My son, Mark, graciously let me move in with him in his tiny apartment in New York City. It helped to be around him and his friends doing *normal* things, rather than sitting around and contemplating my fate. I would be forever grateful for his support, kindness and patience during this major invasion of his privacy. I walked the thirty blocks back and forth to the hospital, which was a good way to distract myself, release tension and get necessary exercise. I also made a point of staying busy visiting friends and family as often as possible.

Stay connected

Don't overlook the importance of maintaining contact with your children, friends and coworkers. If you plan to be hospitalized or receive treatments out of town, talk to your children about how you plan to communicate with them via phone, e-mail, text, Facebook or other social media, or in person—and how often. This will make your absence less stressful for you, and your children and you will have something you can all look forward to.

Throughout my radiation treatments, I travelled

home most weekends, unless my husband and younger son were able to visit. It was important for us to maintain a close relationship by staying in touch and sharing the things happening in our day-to-day lives. We shared many a joke over my hearing loss and uncooperative taste buds. Our time together wasn't sullen but uplifting and filled with good ideas about what we were going to enjoy when all this was "over for Mom." I enjoyed hearing about their attempts to step up and manage many of the household chores on their own in an effort to "keep things under control."

To help connect me with my colleagues and friends back home, one of my dear friends, Debbie, from the school where I worked sent me off with a great collection of movies and a small, portable player that I could use anytime and anywhere. She also stayed connected with me though e-mails and texts, and she shared them with my friends and colleagues back at work. At times, she asked questions about how to handle a situation with a student; I was happy to get involved, which made me still feel useful to the school in some way. I will always be highly grateful for her thoughtfulness and kindness, and she will remain my lifelong friend.

Conclusion

A cancer diagnosis marks the beginning of a very personal journey. Each person has a unique set of values, beliefs and ways of coping with such a devastating illness. You need to allow yourself time to find the best way that works for you and your family.

Each day, you will grow stronger, more courageous and will discover an inner strength you didn't think you had. You'll begin to experience yourself as a much more resilient person. You will find that you become less reactive toward the day-to-day trivial experiences and dwell on the negative a lot less. You'll learn to avoid negative people and look more for the positives. You'll certainly come to appreciate the good things you have in your life and become more grateful toward the people you love.

Throughout your difficult journey, you must have confidence in your doctors and strongly believe that "cancer" no longer equates with "death." You have to be able to say to yourself, "Yes! Cancer may kill me, but I can also live." Be willing to redefine yourself, your priorities as an individual and reconnect with significant people who are important to you. Focus on the day-to-day joys and pleasures in your life, and take time to show appreciation to those who care about you.

I will never forget when I called my close friend,

Penny, with much hesitation, to tell her about my cancer. She had lost a close friend of hers to the disease several years before, and I certainly didn't want her to experience any more sadness. She immediately offered to go with me to New York and help me through the treatments. Needless to say, that was not necessary, but I will always treasure her generous gesture of caring and kindness. She stayed active and tremendously helpful throughout my treatment. Somehow, Penny always knew when I needed an encouraging word, a joke, or a celebration. When I returned home, she came to see me right away. Over a lovely brunch, she gave me a beautiful gold butterfly necklace with a card that said, "The butterfly represents your freedom from the radiation treatments."

I will also never forget my husband's thoughtfulness. The day I was packing to leave for New York, he gave me a small iPod onto which he had loaded all my favorite songs. He said, "This is for those times when you may have to wait for your treatments and I can't be there to hold your hand." These are the moments in life that you imprint on your heart forever.

When I completed my treatment, I returned home to a house full of my close friends and family. The really festive atmosphere kept me from flooding with tears over the reality that I was finally home. Instead, I focused on catching up with everybody and thanking each one personally for their help and support.

Most importantly, I was so touched that it had all been planned and organized by my youngest son without anyone's help. He had taken up so much responsibility in my absence and had handled it so well.

I feel so reassured that, as a family, we have been through such a valuable preparation for facing any emotional challenges that may lie ahead with greater self-confidence and certainly with a lot more love and appreciation for each other's strengths.

Resources

Take the time to check out websites before approaching your child about them. Remember, it's always best, when looking up such delicate information, to do it together with your children to make sure the material provided is suitable and age appropriate. Supporting your children while you're going through your cancer treatment is not going to be easy, and no one should expect to do it perfectly.

When you need more information or have a specific question that needs immediate attention, you can contact the National Cancer Institute hot line for answers to cancer-related questions in English and Spanish. The toll-free number is 1-800-4-CANCER (1-800-422-6237) and is available Monday through Friday, from 9 a.m. until 9 p.m., EST. In addition, the American Cancer Society offers a toll-free Cancer Helpline you can reach by calling 1-800-227-2345. You can expect a trained Cancer Information Specialist to respond seven days a week, 24 hours a day.

Resources

American Cancer Society — Adults can look up "Coping with Physical & Emotional Changes" and "Helping Children When a Family Member Has Cancer: Dealing with Treatment." **www.cancer.org**

Planet Cancer has launched the social networking community, My Planet, which hosts blogs, forums and groups for young adults with cancer. Search under the tab titled Cancer Support, then choose the Caregivers section, which will lead to the Children & Families articles. **http://myplanet.planetcancer.org**

Cancer Care provides free, professional support services and financial help for parents and children dealing with cancer. It also provides helpful information about ways to help children understand cancer. Choose the Ask Cancer Care button, then select Children from the drop-down topic list, for experts' answers to children's frequently asked questions. **www.cancercare.org**

Through the **Macmillan Cancer Support** website, you can obtain two useful booklets about what to tell children when an adult has cancer and how to help them cope.

Select Information and Support, then click on Resources and review the list of publications available, including Information for Teachers and Schools. **www.macmillan.org.uk**

Camp Kesem, organized by college students, is a weeklong, sleepaway summer camp for children ages six to eighteen with a parent who has or has had cancer. The free-of-charge camps are held on college campuses throughout the U.S. Kids participate in camp activities, such as sports, arts and crafts, and drama to give campers a fun filled week while also participating in Cabin Chats with other children and counselors, giving them a chance to share their experiences with each other. **www.campkesem.org**

Kids Konnected provides friendship, understanding, education and support for youth with a parent or caregiver affected by cancer. Support groups for children six to eighteen are guided by licensed therapists and utilize art, writing, games, discussions and peer support. They also offer a chat room. Kids Connected Junior Camp is open to youth, ages seven to thirteen. Go to **kidskonnected.org** or email them at **info@kidskonnected.org** for a group near you.

Resources

About the Contributors

Patricia P. Gage, Ph.D.

Dr. Patricia Gage began her career as a school psychologist and learning specialist with the Bureau of Cooperative Educational Services in Nassau County, New York. In 1991, she moved to Stuart, Florida, where she was instrumental in developing a number of successful programs for children, including the Mainstream Instructional and Behavioral Consultation Program for the Martin County School District, Weebiscus, an early learning program for Hibiscus Children Center and The Academic Center at The Pine School. While working as a school psychologist for the Martin

Patricia P. Gage, Ph.D.

About the Contributors

County School District and later at The Pine School, Dr. Gage enjoyed a busy private practice specializing in psycho-educational evaluations and interventions for students with learning and behavioral issues. Dr. Gage is currently in private practice, in Stuart, Florida, where she specializes in psycho-educational evaluations and interventions for students with learning and behavioral issues.

Dr. Gage has been a member of the Board of Directors of the Rotary Club of Stuart, serving as Literacy and Grants Chair, and a member of the Advisory Council for the Martin Health Foundation. She served as President of the Board for Hibiscus Children Center, President of the Board of Trustees for The Pine School, and as a Mental Health Consultant for Head Start. She continues to serve as a student advisor for the Congressional Award for service.

She is the founder of Women In Philanthropy, a women's philanthropic circle that helps to start programs that promote wellness and mental health for women and children. She was named 2003 and 2010 Rotarian of the Year and was honored as a Woman of Distinction by Soroptimist International in 2003. Currently, she is a member of both the National Association of School Psychologists and the American Psychological Association.

As the cofounder of Hang In There, a company dedicated to providing resources for busy parents, she has coauthored numerous guides on parenting education, addressing topics such as sleep, potty training, charting a child's development, temper tantrums, anxiety, dealing with loss, fostering optimism, and learning strategies for teens. She is the recipient of the gold 2016 Mom's Choice Award for both Hang In There Parenting Cards: *On-the-Go Guides for Raising Infants & Newborns* and *On-the-Go Guides for Raising Toddlers*.

Dr. Gage received her Bachelor of Arts degree in Elementary Education and Psychology from Hunter College, CUNY, New York. She holds a master's degree in School Psychological Services and a Ph.D. in Child/School Psychology from New York University. She is married to a cardiologist, Dr. Joseph Gage, and is the proud mother of two sons, Mark and Christopher.

Learn more about Patricia Gage at:

www.BrainSmartAcademics.com

Christopher J. Gage

Christopher J. Gage

Christopher is an Assistant State Attorney for Florida's 8th District. He earned his Bachelor of Arts degree from Drexel University and his Juris Doctor degree from the University of Florida Levin College of Law.

As a student, he traveled abroad to China, Russia, France, England, Germany, Greece and Italy. He enjoys learning about new cultures, reading, playing flag football and lacrosse, and most importantly, coaching the University of Florida Mock Trial Team.

Marlo Garnsworthy

Marlo Garnsworthy is an Australian-American author, illustrator, editor, writing teacher, and nature lover. Her published works include fiction and nonfiction, though nonfiction and science are her passion. She also works with polar scientists as a science communicator and Outreach Officer in Antarctica on research cruises. She lives in Rhode Island, with her husband, daughter, and a boxer dog named Phoebe.

Marlo Garnsworthy

Learn more at: www.IceBirdStudio.com

Made in the USA
Coppell, TX
22 July 2025

52225114R00075